CW00521356

The Lost Girl: Unearthing the Shadows.

DENNY REYNARD

Published by Denny Reynard, 2023.

This is a work of fiction. Similarities to real people, places, or events are entirely coincidental.

THE LOST GIRL: UNEARTHING THE SHADOWS.

First edition. November 7, 2023.

Copyright © 2023 DENNY REYNARD.

ISBN: 979-8223466741

Written by DENNY REYNARD.

Also by DENNY REYNARD

Introduction

Detective James O'Connor had seen it all in his twenty-five-year career with the NYPD. Murders, kidnappings, and countless other atrocities had passed through his hands. He'd been a relentless force of justice, stopping at nothing to bring criminals to account. But there was one case that had eluded him for over a decade, one that had never left his mind, haunting his every step – the disappearance of his own daughter, Emily.

It was a crisp autumn evening when Emily vanished without a trace. She was just a sweet, innocent girl of ten, the apple of her father's eye. Her laughter had filled their home, and her bright eyes held the promise of a future yet to be written. But in an instant, all of that was shattered. The world turned cold, and James's life descended into darkness.

For years, he had searched tirelessly, turning over every stone, chasing down every lead, but the case had gone cold. He had lost hope of ever finding his daughter until that fateful day, a mysterious clue arrived at his doorstep. It was a small, unassuming package, and inside, a single photograph that sent shivers down his spine. It was an image of Emily, grown and unrecognizable, standing beside a sinister-looking man. On the back of the photograph, a cryptic message: "The Cult of the Lost."

This was the break he had been waiting for, the spark that reignited the fire in his heart. With newfound determination, he delved into the depths of the unknown, into a world filled with secrets, lies, and darkness. The journey to find his daughter would test the limits of his resolve and the boundaries of his sanity.

1

Chapter 1: A Father's Desperation

The photograph, with its frayed edges and colors slightly muted by the relentless passage of time, rested solemnly upon the aged wooden desk. Within the dimly illuminated chamber, Detective James O'Connor regarded it intently, his heart bearing a profound burden that had steadfastly remained for over a decade. Despite his twenty-five years in the service of the NYPD, where he had encountered a litany of horrors, none had ever penetrated his very soul with the potency of his daughter Emily's inexplicable disappearance.

The case had tormented him, dominating his every waking thought and entering his nightmares at night. The obsessive hunt for answers had led him down innumerable dead ends, leaving him with nothing but unanswered questions and a lingering feeling of shame. He had questioned every move he had taken that fatal night, repeating the events over and over in his mind, anxiously seeking any hint he could have missed. But no matter how hard he tried, the truth remained elusive, sliding through his fingers like sand.

On a crisp fall day, as the leaves dropped in a shower of golden brilliance, he had accompanied Emily to the park. Her laughter had filled the atmosphere—a symphony of innocence—as she delightedly flung slices of bread to the ducks serenely gliding upon the pond. Her bright eyes, vast as the skies, conveyed the promise of an unwritten future. Her small hand grasped his, their fingers entwined in a tie that transcended ordinary flesh and blood.

Yet, in the flash of an eye, she was gone, and the world turned into an abyss of cold, impenetrable blackness. He stood paralyzed, his pulse thumping in his chest as dread clutched his every nerve. The park that was once packed with vivid colors and the sounds of youngsters playing now seems dreadfully lonely. Desperate, he yelled out her name, his voice booming through the quiet, but there was no answer. Frantically, he explored every nook and cranny and every hiding location, hoping to catch a glimpse of her golden locks or hear her joyful giggle. But all he discovered was an unsettling quiet that seemed to mock his sorrow.

Time seemed to stretch on forever, each passing second heightening his terror. The fear of losing her and never seeing her again gripped him. Every worst-case scenario played out in his thoughts, each one more terrible than the previous. The weight of the quiet weighed down on him, choking him as he pondered whether he would ever locate her. The once-familiar park now seemed like a maze, keeping him in a nightmare he couldn't wake up from.

Panic continuously gnawed at James's chest as the frenetic pursuit began, but it proved unsuccessful. Days went by, weeks merged into months, and, finally, years, without a single sign of his adored Emily. The official inquiry had been extensive, headed by unshakable policemen who explored every crevice of the park, questioned witnesses, and methodically evaluated even the tiniest hint. Nevertheless, the trail became cold, like an ephemeral phantom escaping past their grip.

James clung to the vague hope that his daughter might one day emerge, coming from the shadows into his arms. However, the image before him had successfully demolished that frail optimism. It featured Emily, however, not the charming kid he remembered; she had turned into an unrecognizable young lady. Her once-brilliant eyes had dimmed, their light pilfered by an unseen malevolence. Beside her stood a guy whose presence projected an atmosphere of gloom.

His countenance was unknown, an intriguing invader in the complex tale of his daughter's abduction. Nevertheless, the ominous aura coming from him was certainly evident, sending chills flowing down James's spine. James couldn't help but worry about what had happened to Emily and how she had fallen into the grips of this mystery guy. The air surrounding them seemed thick with secrets, leaving James with a sickening sensation that finding the truth would not be an easy feat.

He could no longer ignore the fact that Emily had escaped him for far too long—she had not departed freely. She had been abducted and gone from his life. He now had in his quivering hands an image that irresistibly tied her to a frightening realm he had never envisioned. The back of the image contained a mysterious statement, inscribed in large, angular script: "The Cult of the Lost." Those words lingered in the air, burdened with an atmosphere of ambiguity, like a foreboding storm on the horizon. James noticed a cold unrelated to the room's temperature.

As he gazed at the image, James could feel the weight of the unknown weighing down on him. The enigmatic message appeared to hint at truths that he was not yet ready to grasp. It was as if a door had been opened to a world he never knew existed, and now he stood on the cliff, unsure of what lay beyond. The words "The Cult of the Lost" rang in his head, evoking a combination of interest and anxiety inside him. What type of cult was this? And why had they targeted Emily? Questions filled his brain, mixing with an increasing

He realized that he was standing on the edge of something deep, something capable of upending everything. At that moment, he made an unsaid pledge to himself. He would not rest until he unraveled the enigma of the cult and discovered the destiny of his daughter. This signified his second chance—an opportunity to dive into the unknown, to journey into the murky depths of the human psyche, where solutions may exact a terrible price. He understood that this voyage would not be simple and that the way ahead would be perilous. But propelled by a father's love and an unquenchable hunger for knowledge, he steeled himself for what lay ahead. With each step he took, he could feel the weight of his resolve building, pulling him onward into a realm where darkness and illumination danced on a razor's edge.

With the snapshot clasped tenaciously in his quivering fingers, James stood from his chair, his thoughts a maelstrom of determination. He realized he could not tackle this adventure alone. He needed aid, and he knew precisely where to get it. For years, he had collaborated with Detective Sarah Turner, his greatest friend and confidant. Together, they had solved numerous cases, with their intuition and unflinching trust establishing an indestructible relationship.

As he entered Sarah's office, James could feel the weight of his choice on his shoulders. The destiny of their next investigation, which held the key to unraveling a web of lies and corruption, rested in their hands. With a strong knock on the door, James entered, catching Sarah's steady stare. Without speaking a word, he extended the image toward her, their nonverbal language communicating the urgency and seriousness of the situation. With a knowing nod, Sarah accepted the silent appeal, their united resolve sparking a flame of hope in their hearts.

As he put on his coat, James couldn't help but think about how life had completed a full circle, like a ship traveling through turbulent seas. He had gone from being the one seeking justice to being chased, persistently following after illusive characters and the presence of a covert society. This voyage seemed like a plunge into darkness, and he was determined to sink into its depths without hesitation.

His head was flooded with many ideas and a torrent of emotions, but there was one thing that never wavered—an unbreakable love for Emily. This love worked as a continual source of direction during his most difficult periods, lighting his way like a guiding light in the darkness. Now, as he moved into an uncharted and unfamiliar country, this love would continue to be his guiding force, gleaming like a beacon in the distance. In this voyage, a picture became his trusty compass, pointing him toward his final destination—the enigmatic Cult of the Lost.

As he drew closer to the exit, he could feel his pulse thumping in his chest, like a parent anxiously seeking a solution. The snapshot, a basic hint, had inspired a powerful drive inside him. He was resolved to conquer all hurdles, unearth any hidden truth, and face any malevolent presence. He was ready for the terrifying challenge that awaited him. He recognized that the link between a father and his daughter was indestructible, even in the face of the most terrible dangers hidden in the darkness.

Chapter 2: The Mysterious Clue

When Detective James O'Connor exited his apartment, he reached the crowded streets of New York City. Carrying the image felt weighty, always reminding him of the perplexing conundrum that devoured his existence. This city has long been a location where hidden mysteries and undiscovered riddles flourish. However, now he aimed to find the deepest and most crucial one—the cryptic Cult of the Lost.

As Detective James O'Connor traveled farther into the busy thoroughfares of New York City, he couldn't help but absorb the energy surging through the lively streets. Every stride he made seemed to resound with resolve and wonder. With the weight of the portrait pushing on his breast, it acted as a constant companion, both a physical reminder and a metaphorical representation of the riddle that had taken hold of his whole life.

New York City, with its towering skyscrapers and intricate streets, has long been a mesmerizing city, brimming with hidden truths hovering just under its shimmering surface. It was a location where secrets mixed with the fascinating symphony of modern life, generating a tapestry of intrigue and mystery. Detective O'Connor had long been aware of this subtle dance between truth and deceit, but never before had he begun on a quest as significant as the one before him—the revealing of the enigmatic Cult of the Lost.

Guided by an insatiable hunger for truth, O'Connor's objective expanded well beyond the domain of conventional research. It was a voyage into the depths of a clandestine realm, where the shadows whispered old secrets and hidden societies thrived. The Cult of the Lost, steeped in myth and tradition, was a conundrum that had gone unresolved for millennia. Legends tell of its members knowing forbidden knowledge, manipulating strings from the shadows, and wielding inconceivable power.

With each passing instant, the detective's determination was reinforced. He was determined to unravel the closely woven tapestry of the cult's existence and expose its secrets to the light of day. The photograph in his possession held the key—a gateway to uncovering their hidden lair and unmasking the faces behind the enigmatic organization. O'Connor's feet grew more deliberate, his eyes scouring the busy masses for any indications or signals that might take him closer to the truth.

The New York Metropolis, a metropolis of hopes and ambitions, has now become the scene for a war between darkness and light. Detective O'Connor, armed with his unshakeable will and burning curiosity, dug further into the maze of clues and symbols, aiming to expose the truth that lay asleep inside the heart of the city. With each stride he took, the city's pulse echoed in unison with his own, as if propelling him along on his search for truth and justice.

And so Detective James O'Connor marched on, his path lighted by the flickering streetlights and the unrelenting fire inside his spirit. The riddle of the Cult of the Lost awaited its eventual unveiling, and he, armed with unflinching resolve, would not rest until the cloak of mystery was removed and the truth set free.

The cryptic word engraved on the back of the picture reverberated in his thoughts, like a riddle that hadn't been solved yet, only waiting for the solution. He didn't believe in superstition, but when he heard the term 'cult,' he couldn't resist feeling a shudder go down his spine. It was a curious sensation, stuck between rationality and something beyond comprehension.

Despite his mistrust of issues of superstition, the mysterious inscription inscribed on the back side of the image continued to be a fascinating conundrum in his mind. It resembled an unsolved riddle, patiently awaiting its moment of unveiling. The mere utterance of the phrase 'cult' produced a unique emotion, forcing a delicate balance to be established between logic and the world of the supernatural. The unexplainable shudder that coursed down his spine served as a heartbreaking reminder that there are levels of life that are beyond easy explanation.

As he pondered the mysterious statement printed on the back of the image, its deep resonance continued to occupy his mind, much like an elusive problem seeking solutions. His unshakeable skepticism of superstitions did not decrease the unpleasant impact created by the introduction of the term 'cult.' It was as if some ethereal force, merging the worlds of reason and the otherworldly, tiptoed along the fragile brink of his awareness. The intriguing attraction of the letter persisted, stimulating his interest and prompting a great feeling of wonder. With each passing instant, the conundrum became deeper, cloaked in an atmosphere of mystery that resisted simple interpretation.

The chilly feeling that serpentined down his spine served as a terrifying reminder that the frontiers of human comprehension are subject to being breached by unexplainable events. To comprehend the subtleties intertwined with the message, his mind began on an intellectual adventure. Armed with logic as his compass, he explored the labyrinthine hallways of thought, putting together the shards like a skilled detective decoding a puzzling case. For he knew that beneath the folds of this conundrum, a revelation awaited—a revelation that may perhaps transform his perspective of reality.

With every passing instant, the mysterious phrase on the back of the image increased in importance, gripping his imagination with an irresistible appeal. Its enigmatic character appeared to resist rapid understanding, functioning as a siren's lure to uncover its hidden mysteries. Despite his unwavering skepticism towards superstitions, the simple uttering of the term 'cult' sent a shudder through his body traversing the delicate line between reason and the supernatural.

The message, an unresolved conundrum engraved on his mind, encouraged him to go on a quest of exploration. Eager to grasp its mysterious meaning, he entered a domain of intellectual study, his mind comparable to that of a tireless detective in pursuit of truth. Guided by the compass of logic, he methodically studied the complexities of each sign and subtlety inside the encrypted message, like an archaeologist gently sweeping away layers of dirt to expose a buried relic. Within the labyrinthine passageways of his brain, a tapestry of thoughts and speculations started to take form, intertwining threads of possibility and supposition.

The unsettling feeling that resonated down his spine was a tribute to the enigma's deep-rooted power, like echoing old stories from faraway worlds. It prompted him to extend his vision and accept the thought that the limitations of human comprehension are just frail walls in the face of the unfathomable forces that govern our existence. Yet within the joy of this intellectual endeavor, a strong feeling of humility formed. As he battled with the riddles and mysteries, he concluded that certain enigmas are created to stretch the boundaries of human cognition, permanently escaping total decipherment.

And so, engaged in the captivating dance between reason and the unexplained, he resumed his search for enlightenment, propelled by the ravenous yearning to unravel the mysterious mysteries conveyed by the cryptic message that had captured his entire soul.

Detective Sarah Turner had agreed to meet at their treasured refuge, a modest coffee shop discreetly situated in a distant corner of the metropolis. It has been the scene for several talks, both of a professional and personal nature and now it serves as the backdrop for a new chapter in their union. The door's bell rang as he entered, and there she sat, sheltered in the corner, her warm grin a comforting sight among the city's icy detachment.

With a welcome gesture, she drew him closer. James slipped into the chair opposite her, his stare unwaveringly fixated on her eyes, and his voice echoed in quiet tones, weighted with urgency noticeable even before he started.

"Sarah, you won't believe what I've uncovered," he continued his tone an admixture of elation and anxiety. Sarah leaned nearer, her curiosity aroused by James' manner. She could feel the weight of his words before they ever left his lips, prompting a flicker of anxiety to cross her face. Eagerly, she pushed him to continue, eager to solve the riddle he had stumbled across.

She leaned forward, her eyes unflinching. "James, you've always had a gift for uncovering the needle in the haystack. What has stirred you so profoundly?"

In response, he uncovered the image, shoving it across the table. Sarah's eyes focused on it, her brow furrowing as she analyzed the picture. James eyed her closely, watching her reply, well aware of the priceless insights she might supply. Sarah's eyes widened as she took in the features of the snapshot, her mind racing with possibilities. The artwork had a secret message, and James knew that Sarah's acute brain would be the key to understanding it. With bated breath, he waited for her to continue, knowing that their teamwork would reveal the truth behind the cryptic mystery they were about to embark on.

After a protracted period, she raised her eyes, locking them with his, emitting a combination of worry and steely purpose. "James, this discovery is a game-changer. We must identify the man in this photograph and fathom the depths of 'The Cult of the Lost.' This may well be our most promising lead in years." James felt a rush of excitement mixed with anxiety as he pondered her words. The weight of duty rested on his shoulders, knowing that their next moves would define the trajectory of their inquiry. The picture in question sat before them, a blurry black-and-white snapshot that had within it the secrets they sought. They had committed their lives to deciphering the secrets of the unknown, but this particular riddle appeared to carry importance beyond anything they had experienced before. The Cult of the Lost talked about in hushed tones among the most seasoned investigators, was cloaked in myth and folklore.

He confirmed with a nod, feeling a flood of thankfulness for Sarah's unfailing support. Together, they had been an unbeatable team, and he knew their relationship would be the driving force in their quest for the truth. However, depending only on a partnership may lead to biases and a lack of impartial analysis, thus hampering their capacity to identify the truth.

The little but pleasant café was packed with customers conversing and servers dashing to and fro, everyone going about their business without any notion of the perilous and difficult task that the group sat in the corner booth was contemplating. The gang chatted in low whispers as they planned and strategized, agreeing between themselves that putting down the dark cult that had lately appeared in their town was equivalent to attempting to track down a deadly snake concealed in the grass, ready to strike at any time. Their first step in devising a strategy was to attempt to determine the identity of the enigmatic guy seen in the blurry image they had gotten, which looked to show him engaged in some type of ritual.

James, the tech specialist among them, had already improved the picture as much as he could and put it through the facial recognition software down at the police department, hoping to find a match against known offenders in their databases. But the man's features were concealed just enough to make a definitive identification impossible. The irritation was obvious on the faces around the table, but they were determined to keep chasing every clue before the cult could vanish back into the shadows. There was too much at risk for them to fail.

Days passed, and James got a call from a fellow investigator, an excellent scientist. He supplied a name—Victor Halden, a name that bore no immediate importance in James's mind. He scrawled it onto a piece of paper, a weird anxiety creeping over him. Victor Halden functioned as the first jigsaw piece, a gateway leading to the terrible world of the cult.

Now that they had a name to work on due to the face recognition software finally obtaining a match, the gang enthusiastically plunged into studying Victor Halden's past, hoping to discover more about who he was and what ties he could have that might explain his participation with the nefarious cult. It rapidly became evident that Halden was no run-of-the-mill criminal; he seemed to have no previous record of crime whatsoever, and there was very little information to be obtained regarding his past or present actions.

It seemed as if this guy had suddenly emerged out of thin air one day, his sole purpose being to assist in the nefarious goals of the cult. There were no records of former locations, past jobs, or family links; it was as if he had come straight from the shadows, leaving no sign of his life before teaming up with the mystery gang that was now threatening the town. The absence of any concrete information triggered even more red lights for the crew.

What type of individual could manage to keep so utterly unseen and untraceable until now? The gaps in Halden's past produced an uncomfortable impression, like peering into an impenetrable hole where solutions should be. But they had gone too far to give up and were more determined than ever to find the truth about Halden, the cult, and whatever evil machinations they were cooking against the innocent citizens. There had to be some clues, some trail they could pick up, that would disclose Halden's terrible background and genuine goals.

The crew carried on with their inquiry, combing over every piece of material they could find relating to Halden and his known affiliations. There has to be some thread they could tug on that would unravel the mantle of mystery around him. A guy this competent at hiding his traces must have let some information leak eventually. They widened their search, seeking any abnormalities or patterns that corresponded with the cult's recent activity. With lives in danger, failure was not an option. They would learn the truth about Halden and the danger he represented i they had to labor day and night. His secrets could not remain hidden forever.

The group's exhaustive attempts to delve into Victor Halden' background and understand more about who he truly wa disappointingly turned out to be of virtually little benefit or interest On the surface, it looked like Halden had lived an incredibly normal typical life, doing some nondescript office job that made no impact or anybody and living in a tiny, basic apartment that revealed no particula personality or special hobbies. He appeared to merely float through life silently, never aiming for anything exceptional or creating any type o effect along the way.

Looking at Halden's unexceptional background, it was impossible to imagine how he could be engaged in anything as dangerous as the cult that had arisen. But James continued to have an unsettling, nagging sensation that there was more to Halden hiding behind that bland exterior. Something about him still didn't sit right. Though he had attempted to cloak himself in the trappings of an average man, James sensed Halden was not what he looked like. There were too many inexplicable gaps and too many questions left unanswered about who this guy truly was under the surface and what had led him down this dark road into the cult's hands.

James could not let go of the notion that Halden had purposefully developed this innocent, commonplace character as a cover for far more evil motives and goals. They had barely scratched the surface o deciphering the actual enigma of the guy. James was resolved to keep researching, sure that Halden's secrets would disclose the key to comprehending the danger presented by the cult. There has to be some secret fact left to unravel that would disclose Halden's genuine objectives and explain his hidden depths.

James resolved to go back to the beginning and re-examine every minute element of Halden's background, leaving no stone unturned. There has to be some anomaly—some break in the façade of normality Halden had erected. James pored through work records, housing leases, bank statements—any paper trail the guy had left behind. He contacted former neighbors and colleagues again, pressing them harder for any shred of remembrance. Halden was only a ghost until now, but ghosts always left echoes and traces. James would find those remaining shards of Halden's actual character, showing the invisible menace this guy posed. He would not rest until the complete truth was brought to light.

In their quest for intelligence, they reached out to informants, delving into the city's subterranean world, grasping at any fragment of information concerning Victor Halden and 'The Cult of the Lost.' The information they amassed was a mosaic, woven from half-truths, rumors, and hushed murmurs—an intricate tapestry composed of society's periphery.

Sarah's eyes narrowed as she pored over the gathered data, her fingertips drawing linkages on a corkboard that now decorated the wall of James's flat. "James, it appears that this cult operates surreptitiously, evading the law's grasp. Whispers allude to peculiar rituals and a concealed society that preys upon the desperate."

James agreed with a somber nod, his mind racing through many possibilities. "We must approach this, Sarah. We must infiltrate this enigmatic cult, understand its motivations, and ascertain the fate of Emily."

Sarah's demeanor went grim, matching the severity of their quest. "But to accomplish that, we will have to assume unfamiliar identities, engage with the shadows, and dance upon the precipice of peril."

As night settled over the city, they understood that their voyage into the heart of darkness had just begun. Victor Halden symbolized the key and 'The Cult of the Lost,' the mysterious lock. The enigmatic hint had created an unshakable zeal inside them, forcing them to pursue it down every twisting alley, negotiate every complex web of deception, and face the unspeakable monsters that buried themselves in the city's center.

Chapter 3: Into the Shadows

The city had always contained a complicated and impenetrable underground, a labyrinth of secrets and lies where nothing was ever as it appeared on the surface. For as long as anybody could remember, there existed in the darkest corners and back alleys a complex network of concealed facts, deceptions, facades, and half-truths that made detecting the true reality of things practically impossible. It was a realm of ambiguity and deception, where the mere concept of objective truth seemed uncommon and transitory. For Detectives James O'Connor and Sarah

Turner remarked that examining the mysterious group known simply as the group of the lost was like stepping right into the heart of this gloomy abyss that lurked behind the city's veneer of normality. It mimicked a drop into the unknown, a dive into alarmingly murky and opaque waters where they could not be sure what hazards or impediments lay waiting under the surface. Peering into the actions of the cult meant seeking to shine a light on a world that essentially did not want light put upon it, a society that lived on the lack of clarity and on preserving a planned ambiguity to mask its actual character and goals.

Each step further into the cult's enigmatic mysteries and rituals seemed like diving blindly into an unending emptiness, uncertain of whether they would find any firm footing or whether the darkness would just swallow them whole. The investigators advanced slowly but methodically, eager to risk obscurity and trickery. Too much was at risk for them to turn back now. They would continue to hunt resolutely for whatever truth could be dragged out of this abyss, bringing it into the light where its genuine shape might finally be exposed.

Detectives James and Sarah's continuous search to learn the truth about Victor Halden, the enigmatic man in the unusual image, had brought them to the extreme fringes of the city, to areas and villages where rumor and hearsay held more weight than cold, hard facts. As they explored each new clue that may shed light on Halden's identity and his link to the dark cult, they found themselves delving farther and deeper into a world where the concrete appeared to dissolve into the ambiguous. In their hunt for answers, they were leaving the realm of evidence and proof behind and entering a place where whispered legends and half-truths snaking through back alleys appeared to conceal any clear reality.

The more they walked down this road after Halden, the more James was reminded of the massive, sophisticated subway system that lay underneath the busy surface streets of the city. Like that subterranean maze of darkened tunnels extending in every direction, this investigation was taking them into unknown, shadowy places buried far from public view, places where it would be all too easy to become disoriented and lost, unsure of which direction led to truth and which led further into darkness and deceit.

They were chasing Halden into a deep underground now, where he might easily slip away into the shadows, vanishing into any one of a hundred different winding paths and false tracks. Like the numerous crossroads and offshoots lying under the tidy grid of city streets, the path behind Halden branched ceaselessly before them, offering either discoveries or dangers around every turn. James understood they would have to proceed carefully, utilizing every hint and whisper as a guide rather than a definitive destination, if they intended to emerge victorious and unearth Halden's secrets in the end.

Their research efforts had discovered disconcerting truths regarding the sect. Rumors hinted at clandestine meetings inside abandoned warehouses on the outskirts of the city, where the selected few were initiated into the cult's nefarious goal. James and Sarah knew that to penetrate this covert society, they needed to adopt new personalities. The shadows held the key, and they were more than prepared to embrace their mysterious depths.

To move closer to their goal, they established new identities. As undercover operatives in a city rich in secrets, they were experts in assuming masks and masking their actual identities while digging into the cult's complicated intrigues. They visited darkly lit bars, where secrets were bartered as if they were cash, and alliances were established inside the susurration of secretive discussions.

In those gloomy regions, they found a broad collection of mysterious personalities, each more incomprehensible than the last. There was Jasper, a slim figure with a fondness for perplexing riddles who hinted at the cult's ancient rites with a dark glitter in his eye. And then there was Cassandra, a lady with raven-black hair and piercing green eyes, emanating an air of power and an uncanny aura of control.

The farther they walked into this secret realm, the more they realized that the Cult of the Lost was more than a simple gathering of wayward people; it was a tightly-knit community, connected by a common belief in something terrible and incomprehensible. They worked with a feeling of invincibility, hidden in plain sight. It was like attempting to grab a specter—to grasp something that defied the rules of the physical world.

As days went into weeks, James and Sarah unearthed an assortment of unsettling practices. The group convened inside abandoned warehouses, their meetings cloaked in darkness and mystery. They talked in cryptic enunciations and chants, their voices combining into an uncanny chorus that sent chills down one's spine. The atmosphere was loaded with an unearthly aura, a feeling of something lurking just beyond the bounds of human cognition.

In one warehouse, they bore witness to a ritual that sent a frisson of horror through their very souls. A ring of cult members rang a dimly lit altar, intoning incantations that seemed to contradict the natural order of things. On the altar lay a symbol—an inverted triangle with a spinning vortex at its core. The cult members lifted their hands, their voices rising in unison, as though conjuring powers that were not supposed to be invoked.

What James and Sarah experienced when they attended one of the cult's clandestine meetings appeared to mimic some type of ancient ritual or ceremony—a haunting, spooky dance with powers from beyond the regular world. The cryptic chants, the robes, and emblems, the devotion accorded to their mysterious leader, Victor Halden, and the melancholy music floating into the night—it all suggested civilization and traditions harkening back to the ancient past when belief in supernatural abilities and magic were more popular.

As the investigators knelt there, concealed from view, it dawned on them that they had fallen into something considerably more unsettling and dangerous than they had anticipated. This was no innocuous gathering of eccentrics; this was a community sincerely committed to the devotion of unknown forces and entities beyond the bounds of human awareness.

Their regard for the obscure and their ambition to reach places beyond the physical revealed a fanaticism that may make them capable of deadly, unforeseen acts in service to their otherworldly beliefs. James and Sarah now comprehended that they had unearthed something that went beyond a conventional criminal cult. This was an age-old group that fiercely embraced the dominion of the murky unknown over the solid bounds of reality, which most people accepted.

Who knew what such brains, seized with an intense desire for secret knowledge and touch with strange places, would be pushed to do? All the police knew for sure was that everything about this group held an uneasy, menacing undertone they had not noticed until now. Halden was more than simply a compelling speaker; he was a conduit to forces beyond their comprehension. And he was also dangerous in ways they had just started to fathom.

Crouched unnoticed in the darkness, watching the uncanny ceremony unfold before them, James and Sarah could feel their pulses hammering with a combined sensation of terror and resolve. It was gradually obvious from everything they watched that this mysterious cult was a powerful and deadly foe, and by continuing to explore its operations and secrets, the detectives felt they were walking risky terrain where the smallest error might put their lives in jeopardy.

They were sailing perilous, unpredictable seas now in quest of the truth, knowing all too well that one tiny error might send them falling into the unknown depths. The group has previously demonstrated its readiness to defend its secrets by any means required. Yet despite the foreboding menace that appeared to loom over them, permeating every new twist and turn of the case, neither James nor Sarah contemplated going back or abandoning their goal.

The stakes were simply too high, and they understood that choosing to follow this investigation through was the only path forward if they hoped to finally expose the whole truth about the cult, its leader, Victor Halden, and ultimately what had happened to Emily Hawthorne, the woman whose disappearance had set them on this dark journey, to begin with.

They had decided to pursue monsters and play a terrible game of cat and mouse, veiled in gloom. There was no safe or straightforward road ahead anymore. But they would press on stubbornly, devoted to the end, motivated by a desire to light up the veiled dangers lying inside these rites and secret meetings and to see justice done, no matter how twisted a route they had to tread to get there.

James and Sarah's firm desire to find the truth about the cult and its link to Emily's abduction flared inside them like a flaming light, guiding their way through the increasingly complicated and mysterious labyrinth of this inquiry. The city they called home had always housed two different faces: the bright, lively world of ordinary life carried out under sunny skies and along bustling thoroughfares, and the sinister murky underbelly of secrets and unseen actions taking place in clouded passageways and hidden chambers. For most residents, it was simply that pleasant exterior layer that carried significance or touched their lives.

But for James and Sarah, it was the city's dark, underground world of deceit and mystery that suddenly dominated their concentration. because they knew it was only by descending into that enigmatic maze that they would discover the answers and truth they so relentlessly sought. While ordinary people went about their lives oblivious to the dangers and intrigues carried on beneath their feet, the detectives had crossed over into the city's shadow half, compelled by duty and determination to illuminate the sinister secrets and rituals at the heart of the cult, wherever the path led them.

They felt somewhere in that dark underbelly lay the answers to unravel the conundrum of the Cult of the Lost and its link to the bright, promising young lady who had gone one night without explanation. So they voluntarily went on, motivated by resolve and a yearning for justice. The cult dwelled in darkness, but James and Sarah's unrelenting determination shined like a torch to lead their path until the light of truth could eventually dispel the shadows and expose the answers they had given so much to gain.

With every step they walked further into the darkness, their determination burgeoned, and their connection remained steadfast. They were ready to walk the edge of danger, to traverse the treacherous terrain of the undiscovered, all in quest of the truth and the hope that one day they could liberate Emily from the grips of the nefarious cult.

Their voyage had only just started, and they were committed to following it through to its terrifying end, even if it brought them to the darkest corners of the human brain. The Cult of the Lost had opened a gateway to a world they had never envisaged—a universe of secrets, duplicity, and malevolence that had no boundaries.

Chapter 4: Unraveling the Cult

What had begun as a basic missing person investigation had turned into a complicated and high-stakes dance with forces beyond James and Sarah's experience or understanding. Their continued attempt to penetrate the enigmatic Cult of the Lost in hopes of obtaining answers regarding Emily's fate has taken them on a meandering trip into the very heart of a murky society steeped in veiled truths and esoteric rites. Each step carried them further into a realm running by its mysterious laws and saturated by peril on all sides.

It was as if they had engaged in an intricate dance with darkness itself, full of dizzying twists and changes as more and more secrets were disclosed to them. With every discovery of the cult's disturbing beliefs and activities, James and Sarah felt deeply entangled in an alien environment that defied ordinary reasoning and knowledge. The esoteric symbols, the phantom rites, the respect for Victor Halden as a conduit to magical power—it was an atmosphere that contradicted all the detectives believed they understood about the borders of reality. At moments, it seemed they had slipped entirely into the city's strange underworld, an unsettling universe with its codes and terrible energies.

Yet despite it all, neither investigator offered any evidence of backing down or withdrawing from the task they had selected. Even as the cult and its cryptic operations continued to surround them in darkness, James and Sarah pushed on, propelled by a common sense of responsibility and commitment to reveal the truth, wherever it took them. They happily followed each new trail and solved each new enigma, sinking even deeper into the weird labyrinth this research had become. Somewhere at its center still lay the answers regarding Emily, Halden, and the actual objectives of the Cult of the Lost. Their dance had not yet ended.

The further James and Sarah dug into the mysteries and rituals of the Cult of the Lost, the more James started to conceive of their inquiry as analogous to fitting together a complicated, multifaceted jigsaw. The cult itself was a mosaic of veiled bits and weird, ritualistic actions that at first looked unusual and disjointed. There were the bizarre whispered chants heard through walls, the illuminated meetings in vacant warehouses presided over by Victor Halden, the unfathomable symbols scratched into surfaces across the city, and the esoteric writings and artifacts gathered from members. Each new revelation or clue they unearthed felt sharp and threatening, but it also seemed to create another little fragment of some greater, yet foggy, tapestry. Bit by bit, they were creating a picture that may ultimately make sense of the cult's mission and methods.

Each ceremony observed each rumor chased down, and each coded communication understood provided another missing piece essential to creating the answer this mystery demanded. James believed some critical vision was waiting to be revealed after they gathered and assembled enough pieces from the cult's fragmented mosaic. Incrementally, patterns and forms were starting to emerge from the shadows. The cryptic shards were progressively merging into an elaborate picture that would disclose the actual nature and plans of their foes when finished.

Until then, they had to be patient and relentless, collecting every accessible element from the cult's esoteric ritualism and mythology. Even the tiniest sliver might be the critical piece essential to eventually unravel the big tapestry. They were engaged in a deep but risky puzzle, yet each piece brought hope.

They had succeeded in identifying many crucial members of the cult, among them Victor Halden, the dominant guy in the shot, and Cassandra, the mysterious lady emanating an aura of power. Their involvement in the cult's intrigues remained hidden, like ever-shifting shadows projected onto a wall, elusive and cryptic.

Their next focus point became the cult's rituals—a succession of odd and unnerving rites that appeared to blur the boundaries between the earthly and the otherworldly. In one such incident, James and Sarah had been observers at a ceremony involving the summoning of a shadowy creature, a being that defied any sort of explanation. It was as if they had unknowingly wandered into the pages of a horror book, where the barriers between truth and fiction crumbled into a strange nightmare.

As James and Sarah kept investigating every conceivable trail that may shed light on the Cult of the Lost and its unnerving activities, they started searching out specialists on the occult and esoteric mystical organizations, thinking these academics could help explain the cult's symbols and rituals. This led the investigators deep into dusty libraries and abandoned archives full of old documents referring to mysterious organizations spanning the centuries committed to gaining prohibited or hidden information. It was like going through a convoluted, winding maze of obscure history and ideas.

James and Sarah found themselves gazing over decaying manuscripts, analyzing weird patterns in antique artwork, and reading descriptions of long-ago rituals geared to reaching unknown energies outside the bounds of normal human awareness. They spoke with anthropologists and historians who took them through this esoteric world of lost ancient groups and heretical offshoots from mainstream religions that had embraced the occult.

It was a society in which magical symbols retained power, where ritual chanting and gifts to otherworldly beings were considered means to glimpse the truths concealed beyond reality's frail surface. The more James and Sarah examined this mysterious area of secret rites and cosmic riddles, the more connections they noticed to the Cult of the Lost's activities. Though centuries separated them, the underlying aspirations were aligned—to transcend commonplace life and grasp knowledge conventional society judged hazardous or prohibited.

Navigating these complicated paths of esoteric history and magic needed time and an open mind, but somewhere in this weird maze of arcane knowledge lay the keys to finally making sense of the mysterious cult they were following and its actual goal. The symbols and rituals were signposts; people only had to learn to understand them.

Sarah's investigation had exposed a connection between the cult and a historical person called Malachi Blackwood, a name that sent tremors through the annals of the arcane. Blackwood had been an accomplished scholar of the occult, a man whose writings and experiments had pushed the bounds of human cognition. His name was murmured in quiet respect, comparable to that of a forbidden god, and it appeared the cult believed themselves to be the torchbearers of his poisonous heritage.

Their research uncovered the cult's belief in the presence of parallel dimensions—realms coexisting with our own but disguised from a common view. This notion remained tough for James to understand, analogous to a mirage on the far horizon, always just out of reach. The cult's rituals, it appears, were designed to penetrate the boundaries between these realms, allowing them to harness the power of the mysterious.

However, when they unearthed more of the cult's operations, a plethora of concerns developed. What was the ultimate goal underlying these rituals? What did they seek to accomplish by calling monsters from different dimensions? And, most crucially, did the cult hold the key to revealing Emily's whereabouts?

As they traveled further into this maze of secrets, the looming threat became more evident. They were no longer passive witnesses but active participants in the cult's perplexing rites. The prospect of discovery loomed like a storm on the horizon, prepared to unleash its wrath at any moment.

Their unyielding dedication to the truth and their steadfast intention to find Emily remained unabated. Yet they were completely aware that the route they had chosen was laden with hazards. The cult represented a strong enemy, with its members trapped by an obsessive commitment to its maleficent doctrines. James and Sarah understood that they were treading a cliff of hazards, and the repercussions of their unrelenting pursuit may be deadly.

The expedition into the Cult of the Lost had brought them face to face with the deepest recesses of human conviction—a region where the boundary between reality and the supernatural overlapped. It was a place in which the limits of the known world blurred, and the shadows hid mysteries that eluded reasonable explanation.

With each discovery, they found themselves lured further into the mystery of the cult, much like explorers delving into new ground. The jigsaw was difficult; its parts dispersed, but their drive to put it together and uncover the hidden realities inside the Cult of the Lost remained unrelenting.

Their ensuing path of action was evident—to acquire the confidence of the cult's innermost circle, to become necessary members, and finally to find the answers they so fervently sought. The route ahead was clouded in ambiguity, but they were vividly aware that they had gone too far. The Cult of the Lost had thrown its gloomy shadow over their lives, and they were committed to confronting it, discovering its secrets, and, finally, saving Emily from its depths.

Chapter 5: The Sinister Agenda

The Cult of the Lost had developed as a tangled tapestry of beliefs and rituals, a domain where the borders between the ordinary and the supernatural merged into an unnerving mosaic. Detectives James O'Connor and Sarah Turner had pushed farther into its depths, uncovering a nefarious intent that defied simple explanation.

On a dark summer night, they got an unusual invitation to one of the cult's most covert meetings. The message, enigmatic in nature, was given by a dark messenger who appeared to materialize and dematerialize like a phantom. The cult's fascination had strengthened its grasp on them, and they were unable to resist the pull of the unknown.

When James and Sarah arrived at the location they had been given for the cult's next meeting, they found themselves greeted with a majestic, vast house on the outer outskirts of the city that had been abandoned for decades. With its ancient masonry covered in vines, rows of gloomy windows like the blank eyes of a huge ghost, and continuously barred iron gates, the secluded property had the impression of some abandoned castle from another century, now surviving in a condition of ruin and eerie melancholy.

As the investigators came over the overgrown grounds, they could sense a heavy hush hanging in the air, as if the whole environment were drenched with whispers from the past. There was a definite sensation that they were crossing into a realm that did not belong to the rational, orderly world they knew—some pocket dimension where the norms and logic contemporary civilization ran under no longer applied. Moving around the mansion's huge hallways covered with cobwebs and dust, seeking for the cult members they knew convened here frequently, James and Sarah both grappled with the eerie impression that they were trespassers in a domain entirely beyond their understanding.

The mysteries these walls concealed and the esoteric rites executed inside these rooms appeared to exceed anything their expertise as investigators had prepared them for. It was like coming into some forgotten culture with habits and knowledge well beyond one's understanding. Yet they could not turn back now when solutions could lie close.

Gripping their anxiety, James and Sarah opted to continue farther inside the decaying home, deducing that the cult must have picked this strange spot for a purpose. Some critical clue awaited them if they could bear the stifling atmosphere pressing on their shoulders. They must stay watchful, examining everything while attempting not to disturb the shadows.

Inside the house, a large hall was bathed in soft illumination. Cult members, wrapped in black robes, walked with somber intent. The mood was imbued with strange expectations, comparable to the quiet before a rising storm. In the middle of the chamber sat an elevated platform bearing an exquisite altar.

James and Sarah absorbed themselves into the cult members, their hearts beating with the knowledge that they were on the verge of exposing the core of the cult's nefarious objective. The rites they had watched earlier had been unnerving, but this one threatened to reveal something far more terrible.

The cult's leader, a person with an intimidating presence with a voice that carried like a sinister incantation, climbed the stage. He controlled the proceedings like a maestro orchestrating a horrific symphony, influencing the acts of his ardent followers with delicate gestures. His eyes shone with a fanatical fire, and his words carried the attraction of a siren's song, luring his followers farther into the abyss.

Before them in a cleared glade, two dozen robed people had set themselves in a large circle around a primitive stone altar. Their faces were shrouded by hoods, but the flickering firelight glinted off eyes that blazed with fevered desire. As one, the cult members started to chant their voices rising in a discordant chorus of lost souls, screaming out to things best left undisturbed. At the middle of the blood-stained altar lay the sacrificial offering—a little lamb, its innocent eyes wide with dread Its legs had been shackled to prevent escape from the awful end that awaited.

James felt a stab of empathy for the pitiful thing, so young and oblivious of the profane purpose to which its little existence would be committed. Slowly, the robed leader walked forward to assume his position at the altar's head. His chin was lifted, showing a maniacal smile pulled tight over his emaciated face. In his hands, he clutched a curved blade forged from basic metal, its edge polished to a deadly razor sharpness. With a frightening swiftness born of habit, the cultist swept the sword down in a huge arch.

Crimson poured forth as the lamb's neck was opened in a gruesome show. Its bleating scream was suddenly cut short. Dark magic was going to be loosed upon the earth that night, and one innocent would pay the ultimate price to see it done. James and Sarah watched on in silent horror, bearing helpless witness to the ritual's sinful culmination.

The meaning of the rite was apparent. The group clung to their belief in the power of sacrifice, allowing the innocent to satisfy its demonic forces. It was a concept steeped in ancient rituals, an unsettling reminder of a period when humans had attempted to deal with powers beyond their knowledge.

James and Sarah, as they bore witness to this horrible scene understood they had to maintain their cover to continue unraveling the cult's deadly purpose. They murmured the chants and engaged in the rites, their hearts weighted down by the load of dishonesty.

The cult's aim extended beyond rituals and sacrifices. They believed in the presence of parallel dimensions—worlds coexisting with our own, hidden from the perspective of the ordinary. Their objective was to penetrate the boundaries between these realities, gaining access to prohibited knowledge and power.

The cult's leader talked about creatures existing in these parallel dimensions—beings of incredible strength and malevolence. They were like old gods, oblivious to humanity's misery. Yet, the cult thought that by pleasing these beings, they might harness their power and remake the world according to their perverted wants.

James and Sarah couldn't help but draw similarities to old myths and stories when humans strove to gain favor with deities via sacrifices and ceremonies. The cult's ideas were a twisted perversion of these age-old legends, a horrific retelling of humanity's drive for power and knowledge.

The cult's reach went beyond its ceremonial acts. They were engaged in a labyrinth of unlawful enterprises, from extortion to money laundering, all meant to fuel their nefarious objectives. It was as if they were establishing an empire of evil, concealed in plain sight, and James and Sarah were determined to smash it.

As they probed more into the cult's purpose, they came to learn that they were dealing with a foe unlike any they had fought before. The cult's power and influence were extensive, and its adherents were staunch in their allegiance. James and Sarah were like moths lured to a flame, entangled in the web of darkness produced by the cult.

When they left the house that night, a sensation of dread filled their heads. The cult's evil mission was a tremendous force, and they were now more firmly embedded in its web than ever. The way ahead was hazardous, but they understood that retreat was not an option. The cult had thrown its shadow over their lives, and they were adamant in their mission to face it, disclose its secrets, and finally liberate Emily from its grasp.

The disclosure of the evil objective had sent chills flowing down their spines, displaying a terrifying reality in the most unnerving way. James and Sarah exchanged concerned looks as the cult leader's statements appeared to pull back the curtain on a plot reaching back through the centuries. According to his rant, the principles of the Order were entrenched in long-forgotten traditions and prohibited behaviors dating back to antiquity. Tales of pagan gods and nameless monsters were spoken in dark corners of the globe, evoking forces best left undisturbed.

The rites done under the light of the moon were meant to establish contact and welcome influence from these mysterious powers. Though dubious, they could not dispute that the leader talked with unusual certainty, as if privy to forbidden information. His ravings plunged them into a murky realm of mystery and terror, flooding their thoughts with weird pictures from a world that lurked just beyond the limits of consciousness. Questions developed that upset their sense of reality, suggesting frightening possibilities regarding the actual nature of life.

That night, sleep would not come easy to the two friends as they tossed and turned, haunted by dreams spawned by the unnerving disclosures. They felt as if the gloss of the commonplace had been taken away, revealing deeper undercurrents in the world. In the cult's unbalanced beliefs, Sarah and James believed they had experienced something unconscionable—a look into the abyss where lunacy and blasphemy dwell.

Their next stages in the inquiry were evident. To destroy the cult and disclose the truth about Emily, they had to maintain their disguise, win the confidence of the cult, and find a method to interrupt their operations. The dark plan had been disclosed, but the war was far from done, and the shadows contained secrets that could only be revealed by unflinching persistence and unbreakable resolve.

Chapter 6: Confronting the Past

The Cult of the Lost has extended its broad, ominous shadow over the lives of Detectives James O'Connor and Sarah Turner. With every discovery about the cult's beliefs and activities, their drive to face the past and disclose its deepest secrets flared like an insatiable fire. The dark intent they had observed had only bolstered their determination because they recognized that the answers they sought were intertwined with the cult's cryptic past.

As they continued their undercover activities inside the cult, James and Sarah couldn't help but be reminded of the group's effect on its members, analogous to a puppeteer masterfully manipulating marionettes. The cult's leader maintained an almost hypnotic grip over his followers, his charm and authority reminiscent of charismatic cult personalities from history, enticing believers with promises of forbidden knowledge and power.

Their involvement in the cult's rites and ceremonies became more personal, with their masks of deceit becoming more difficult to preserve. The boundary between their genuine identities and their assumed personalities blurred, and the weight of their deceit started to take its toll. They were like players on an infinite stage, enacting roles that threatened to engulf them.

Amidst the rites and incantations, James and Sarah sought any hint that might lead them to Emily. The cult had gotten bolder, gradually bringing them into its inner circle. It was amid these sacred meetings that they unearthed signs of a link between the cult's leader and the strange disappearance of James's daughter.

The cult's leader, known as Father Malachai, was a man of intriguing origins and unbounded magnetism. He was like a character from a lost legend, a dark magician who commanded the allegiance of his followers with a just look. James couldn't help but draw comparisons between Father Malachai and the charismatic leaders of history who had led their people down a road of madness and disaster.

As they looked further into the cult's background, James and Sarah found a trail of disappearances, hauntingly similar to Emily's case. The cult had been operating for decades, and its dark mission had left a path of broken lives and devastated families in its wake. The echoes of their previous acts appeared to ricochet down the gloomy hallways of the cult's history.

One name surfaced regularly in the data they uncovered: Victor Halden, the guy from the photos. His link to the cult was deeper than they had previously believed, and it was evident that he had played a substantial part in the group's operations. The pieces of the jigsaw were slowly fitting together, exposing a tapestry of malevolence that reached back into the annals of time.

The cult's fixation with parallel realms and forbidden knowledge appeared to focus on a tome known as the "Blackwood Codex," a dark and ancient manuscript that was said to reveal the secrets of the cult's power. It was like a grimoire from a terrible fairy tale, a book of incantations and rituals that contained the secret to their beliefs and practices.

James and Sarah realized that the Blackwood Codex was the key to unraveling the cult's secrets and knowing the actual nature of their deadly mission. They had to uncover it, face the past, and disclose the evil that had been buried for so long.

Their diligent hunt for clues concerning the mystery codex led James and Sarah to a shocking discovery: buried beneath the bowels of the expansive cult property was a massive, secret library. Hidden underground and warded with mystical barriers, it had remained lost to the outer world for countless decades. As they made their way through secret corridors in the stone walls, the musty air became heavy with the heady weight of collected knowledge. They emerged into a gigantic cavern whose walls and ceilings faded into the blackness far above. Shelves carved from the living rock extended as far as the eye could see, packed with drooping tomes and scrolls wrapped in leather that appeared older than time itself. The library was a place where centuries were made irrelevant. Works from antiquity sat side by side with recent publications, all judged worthy of being buried in this freezing of the passage of years. It felt as if the past and present coexisted here on an infinite continuum. Sarah was struck by the odd impression that the information inscribed inside these volumes had mysteries that transcended common existence. She stroked her fingertips down spines etched with exotic symbols, feeling as if the borders between reality and tale, history and mythology, were made permeable inside these resonating stones. This was the cult's inner sanctum—a junction where lost epochs and unseen worlds collided. James and Sarah knew that behind these barely illuminated stacks were the answers they sought if only they could identify them from the many whisperings of the centuries reverberating in the pregnant blackness.

The codex was claimed to contain the cult's most tightly guarded information, a compendium of rites and incantations that permitted them to cross the boundaries between realms. It was like a forbidden grimoire, a book of shadows that could transform the universe according to the cult's wants.

As they pored over the old document, James and Sarah couldn't help but be reminded of the innumerable stories of forbidden knowledge from literature and mythology. It was as if they had fallen into the pages of a grim tale, a narrative of hubris and the chase of power that eventually led to their ruin.

The codex held the key to the cult's deadly goal, and they knew that they had to obtain it to face the past and disclose the truth that lay concealed inside its pages. The route ahead was laden with peril, and the cult's influence was a continual threat, but they were determined to carry their mission through to its conclusion.

Their trek had brought them into the heart of darkness, where the past and the present blended into an uncanny tapestry of secrets and lies. The cult's deadly objective was like a web, its strands extending back through time, and James and Sarah were determined to unravel it, face the past, and bring Emily back from the abyss.

The Blackwood Codex was their key to the truth, and they were willing to do whatever it took to obtain it. The way ahead was hazardous, but they knew that they had gone too far to turn back. The cult's dark objective had exposed itself in all its malevolence, and they were resolved to face it and uncover the truths that had been buried for far too long.

Chapter 7: The Ties That Bind

In their persistent pursuit of the mysterious Cult of the Lost, Detective James O'Connor and Detective Sarah Turner plunged deeper into a universe steeped with secrets, ancient rituals, and malicious beliefs. The route they had chosen was filled with hazards, but with each discovery, they felt the unseen threads of fate meticulously creating a complicated tapestry that tied them to the deadly cult.

As they continued their undercover investigation, they couldn't avoid the impression that they were linked to the cult by more than simply their responsibilities as investigators. It was as if the strands of destiny had captured them inside the cult's sophisticated web, knitting them into a story that went well beyond the bounds of their professional lives.

The links that tied them to the religion were analogous to the roots of an old tree, digging deep into the annals of history and taking nourishment from the darkness. They grasped that to challenge the cult and lay bare its secrets, they had to know the nature of these linkages and trace them back to their roots.

Their inquiry brought them to the cult's innermost circle, where they discovered individuals whose commitment to the organization ran deep, like a river that had engraved its path through the millennia. It was inside the cult's rituals and meetings that they started to perceive the connection between the past and the present—how old beliefs had been kept and passed down through the generations.

As they witnessed the cult's rites, they couldn't help but draw similarities to the rituals of ancient civilizations, where confidence in the supernatural and the efficacy of sacrifice had been vital to their religious traditions. The cult's links to these time-honored customs were unmistakable, analogous to echoes from a bygone period.

The cult's head, Father Malachai, stood as a defender of these old beliefs, a custodian of evil knowledge scrupulously kept and transferred down the decades. His power inside the sect was total, and his link to the past was incontrovertible. It was as if he had inherited the mantle of a high priest from a long lineage of predecessors, each passing on the flame of forbidden knowledge.

Their attempt to fathom the links that united the cult led them to a collection of ancient documents and manuscripts locked away in a covert room inside the group's headquarters. These texts provided a window into the past, showing the cult's beginnings and the convictions that had formed its malicious mission.

One paper, in particular, piqued their interest. It was a diary scribed by a man called Ambrose Blackwood, an ancestor of the cult's leader. Ambrose Blackwood had been a scholar of the occult, a man whose fixation with forbidden knowledge had driven him to seek out the cult's secrets. His notebook was similar to a window to the past, a chronicle of his journey into the abyss.

As they studied Ambrose Blackwood's reports, they couldn't help but be impressed by the similarities between his search for knowledge and their own. He had been motivated by an insatiable hunger for information and a desire to unravel the mysteries of the cosmos, much like James's unyielding resolve to find his daughter.

The relationships that linked them to the cult's past were becoming increasingly obvious, establishing a tapestry of linkages that reached over time and geography. They discovered that the cult's evil objective was not a new creation but had its origins in a lineage of belief that had been passed down through centuries.

Their grasp of the cult's past gave insight into the nature of their links to the group. It was as if they had been sucked into a tale that had been unfolding for generations—a drama of darkness and forbidden knowledge that had transcended the borders of time.

Armed with this information, James and Sarah were aware that they were now closer to uncovering the cult's secrets than ever before. The linkages linking them to the cult's past were analogous to threads in a complicated tapestry, and they were steadfast in following these threads to their frightening end.

Their inquiry had brought them far into the past, but the route forward remained cloaked in ambiguity. The cult's influence and power were tremendous, and its loyalty to its malicious mission was steadfast. Nevertheless, James and Sarah were similar to detectives of destiny, steadfast in their quest to face the cult, uncover the truth, and follow the threads that tied them to their terrifying destination.

"The Ties That Bind" had blossomed into a wellspring of power for them, acting as a reminder that they were not alone in their journey. They were part of a tale that reached well beyond their own lives, and they were determined to see it through to its frightening finale. The cult's secrets were comparable to a dark labyrinth, and they were steadfast in traversing its hazardous pathways, saving Emily from the abyss, and facing the history that had led them to this vital moment.

Chapter 8: Dangerous Alliances

In the cryptic domain of the Cult of the Lost, partnerships were analogous to illusive threads ingeniously knitting the cult's complicated tapestry of secrets together. As Detective James O'Connor and Detective Sarah Turner persevered in their undercover operation, they found themselves entangled inside a maze of complicated and deadly ties, where devotion and treachery frequently blurred into an invisible line.

The cult's inner circle was a complicated network of ever-shifting ties, where trust proved a fragile and transitory commodity. It resided inside a society where secrets constituted the currency of power and the cult's members participated in a dangerous game of deception and manipulation. The affiliations inside the cult were evocative of an elaborate web of intrigue, where allegiance flowed with the same capriciousness as the tides.

James and Sarah had taken new identities inside the cult, and as they dug more into its inner machinations, they found themselves building their relationships, treading a hazardous tightrope of deceit. They had to gain the confidence of the cult's members to become insiders in a world that lived on society's margins.

Their connection with the sect was a double-edged sword. On one side, it offered them access to the cult's covert rites and meetings, enabling them to watch its inner workings and gain important information. However, on the other hand, it exposed them to the perpetual threat of exposure. The cult's members were extraordinarily competent at detecting duplicity, and a single error might be lethal.

As they traversed the dangerous environment of the cult's inner circle, they couldn't help but be reminded of the alliances established in the annals of history, where political intrigues and power conflicts had irrevocably altered the future of countries. The cult's complex ties resembled a microcosm of that world, a network of links that held the secret to its nefarious objective.

The cult's leader, Father Malachai, was a master at creating partnerships, comparable to a puppeteer delicately manipulating the strings of his believers with remarkable precision. His authority over the cult was total, and his ties created a complex fabric of devotion and horror. It was as if he had established an empire of darkness, where his words were law and disagreement was immediately punished.

James and Sarah's affiliation with the cult provided them insights into the organization's deepest workings, allowing them to see its rituals and rites. It was at these sessions that they found thin evidence of a link between the cult's leader and the inexplicable disappearance of James's daughter. They realized that their collaboration with the cult was a hazardous bet, having the potential to either deliver a breakthrough or expose the group's deadly secrets.

The cult's affiliations went beyond its inner circle, going deep into the heart of the city's underbelly. They were enmeshed in a sophisticated web of unlawful enterprises, spanning extortion and money laundering, all aimed at supporting their evil ambitions. These partnerships resembled a covert network of power and influence, an inconspicuous empire that functioned in plain sight.

As they investigated further into the cult's relationships, they identified links to a criminal underworld where alliances and power conflicts maintained dominance. It was a world where loyalties switched continuously and alliances were created and shattered in the blink of an eye. The cult's web of power went well beyond its rites and ceremonies, and its affiliations were threads extending into every nook and crevice of the metropolis.

Their association with the cult had submerged them in a deadly world of secrets and deception, but it had also brought them closer to the truth. They recognized that to face the cult and lay bare its secrets, they had to negotiate the perilous maze of relationships, unraveling the linkages that kept the group's web of secrets intact.

The ties they had built inside the cult were analogous to lifelines in a perilous sea. They were walking a hazardous line, wavering between winning the confidence of the cult's members and keeping their cover. The cult's influence and strength were tremendous, and their affiliation with it was an ever-present source of threat.

Their inquiry had brought them deep into the core of the cult's deadly ties, and the route forward remained cloaked in doubt. The cult's nefarious objective stood as a powerful force, and their union with it was similar to a tightrope walk, needing accuracy.

Their aim remained unambiguous: to destroy the cult's ties, reveal its secrets, and return Emily from the abyss. The friendships they had made inside the cult were keys to the truth, and they stayed unwavering in their desire to carry their mission through to its horrific climax. The risky alliances they had made were analogous to a labyrinth of lies, and they were steadfast in traversing its tortuous chambers, regardless of the hazards involved.

The links that linked them to the cult resembled threads in an elaborate tapestry, and their partnership with the cult served as a continual reminder of the dangers that loomed. Nevertheless, they knew that they had come too far to backtrack and that the cult's relationships held the key to uncovering its secrets. They were resolved to tackle the evil that had caught them inside this convoluted web of intrigue and deceit.

Chapter 9: A Trail of Deception

In their continuous effort to uncover the enigmas of the Cult of the Lost and locate Detective James O'Connor's missing daughter, Emily, the route has turned into a tangled maze of lies. The cult had successfully spun a tapestry of secrets and lies, ensnaring James and Detective Sarah Turner in a world where the illusive truth remained a distant phantasm.

As they persisted in maintaining their secret positions inside the group, it became obvious that lying carried tremendous significance. The cult members sported masks of intense dedication and everlasting commitment, masking their actual motives beneath a veneer of ritualistic intensity. Deception stood as their impenetrable barrier, their armor, and a devastating weapon they wielded with surgical precision.

Father Malachai, the cult's leader, had perfected the art of deceit to perfection. His captivating presence and aura of authority functioned like a magician's sleight of hand, diverting his followers from the truth and further into obscurity. Every word and gesture he said was precisely planned, meant to preserve the façade of righteousness while masking the cult's nefarious objective.

Their grasp of the cult's skill of deceit increased as they witnessed its rituals and meetings. The cult's devotees moved in a choreographed dance of secret, their acts wrapped in symbolism and disguised meanings. Deception was their art, and they resembled performers in a diabolical play, adopting their characters with relentless conviction.

As James and Sarah traversed this domain of deceit, they couldn't help but draw similarities to ancient literature and mythology. The cult's rites and ceremonies matched scenes from a dark opera, where the limits between reality and the supernatural were blurred. Deception arose as a reoccurring element in these stories when gods and humans alike exploited cunning and deceit to attain their purposes.

Their quest for the truth had led them to find a trail of lies that stretched well beyond the cult's rituals. The cult's dark mission surpassed the borders of its inner circle, delving into the heart of the city's underground. It was a place where deceit was the way of life, where friendships were created and destroyed with casual grins, and where the truth was a rare and priceless commodity.

The cult's participation in a network of unlawful operations, ranging from extortion to money laundering, resembled an elaborate tapestry of deceit that spanned across the city. It was a society where the boundary between the criminal and the cultist sometimes blurred and where deceit served as the key to survival.

In the course of their research, James and Sarah discovered a link between the cult and a criminal group known as the Black Serpents. The alliance between these two parties was analogous to a pragmatic partnership, a merger of power and resources that enabled them to achieve their respective interests. The deception worked as the glue keeping this union together, as both forces masked their actual aims beneath a veneer of collaboration.

Their trip had carried them to the center of a society where deceit was the modus operandi, a place where alliances were built and severed in the blink of an eye. It was a world where the truth remained a rare and elusive treasure and where the implications of lying may be lethal.

The trail of deceit they had exposed resembled a sophisticated jigsaw, where one piece connected to another, and the complete image remained tantalizingly beyond grasp. They knew that to face the cult and lay bare its secrets, they must negotiate this arena of deceit with precision and sagacity, following the trail wherever it may lead.

Their research had grown into a fight of wits, a cat-and-mouse game where deceit functioned as the currency of power. The cult's secrets were analogous to a gem hidden deep behind a labyrinth of lies, and they were adamant in their mission to find the truth, regardless of the cost.

Deception developed as the cult's weapon of choice, a powerful enemy indeed. James and Sarah were well aware of the treacherous road they were on and the deadly consequences that lying may bring. Nevertheless, they were steadfast in their vow to pursue the trail of deceit to its frightening end, to face the cult, disclose the truth, and recover Emily from the abyss.

A Trail of Deception had morphed into a deadly quest, as each step pulled them farther into a world of shadows and mystery. The cult's expertise of deceit offered a daunting task, however, their unshakable drive propelled them to traverse it with unyielding resolve. The route ahead remained clouded in ambiguity, but they understood they had come too far to turn back now. The deception was their foe, but the truth remained their ultimate aim, and they were committed to tracking the trail to its terrifying end.

Chapter 10: Beneath the Surface

The Cult of the Lost portrayed itself as an iceberg, hiding its nefarious goals under the surface, with just a portion of its deadly depths visible to the public. As Detective James O'Connor and Detective Sarah Turner maintained their unflinching pursuit, they came to learn that grasping the cult's mysteries meant going beyond the surface and plunging into the murky annals of its past.

Their research voyage had brought them deep into the cult's inner sanctuary, where they bore witness to its ceremonies and convocations. Within these clandestine meetings, cult members zealously intoned incantations and executed mysterious rites. However, it was apparent that these rites were simply the visible tip of the iceberg, the public veneer veiling a much more sinister reality.

As James and Sarah dug beyond the surface of the cult's activities, they uncovered a universe of beliefs and behaviors that seemed to transcend the confines of reason. The cult's preoccupation with parallel realms and forbidden information functioned as a covert undercurrent, pulling them farther into the abyss of the unknown.

Their search had brought them to a collection of old documents and manuscripts stashed beneath a secret room within the cult's headquarters. These records acted as windows into the cult's past, showing a history more deep and intriguing than they had previously guessed. The beginnings of the sect were shrouded in mystery, comparable to a lost tale awaiting disclosure. As they delved deeper into the ancient texts, deciphering cryptic symbols and unraveling hidden meanings, they uncovered a web of connections to historical events and figures that seemed almost too extraordinary to be true. The secrets held within these records hinted at a clandestine power that had influenced the course of history itself, leaving them both fascinated and unnerved by the enormity of what they had stumbled upon.

One specific item drew their attention: a diary made by Ambrose Blackwood, an ancestor of the cult's leader, Father Malachai. Ambrose Blackwood had been a scholar of the occult, and his diary was a portal to a world of forbidden knowledge. As they skimmed its pages, they saw that the cult's fascination with the supernatural had deep-rooted roots, reaching back through the centuries.

The notebook revealed ancient rites and incantations, gateways to alternative realms, and encounters with things from beyond. It was as if they had chanced upon a hidden chapter of history, a tale of darkness and the chase of forbidden knowledge. The cult's actions constituted a modern interpretation of these age-old beliefs, a continuation of a tradition handed down through the millennia.

As James and Sarah explored more into the cult's past, they unearthed a trail of disappearances that had been entwined with the cult's operations for decades. The cult's malignant purpose had left behind a legacy of damaged lives and ruined families, and the echoes of their acts seemed to linger across time. The trail of disappearances resembled a mournful song, a requiem that spoke of the cult's malignancy.

Father Malachai, the head of the cult, had the key to knowing the unfathomable depths of its deadly objective. His link to the cult's past was clear, and his function as a custodian of prohibited information lay at the core of their research. He resembled a modern alchemist, attempting to convert the basic parts of mankind into something bigger, something beyond the grasp of regular people.

The cult's emphasis on the "Blackwood Codex," an old and illegal manuscript, acted as a bridge between the past and the present. This terrible grimoire held the key to their beliefs and rituals, and James and

Sarah knew that acquiring it was crucial to facing the cult's mysteries. The codex resembled Pandora's box, housing the forbidden knowledge the cult hoped to grasp. As James and Sarah delved deeper into their investigation, they discovered that the cult's obsession with the Blackwood Codex went beyond mere curiosity. The manuscript held ancient spells, incantations, and dark secrets that had been passed down through generations. It was rumored to contain the power to unlock hidden dimensions, summon otherworldly entities, and even grant immortality. The cult believed that by deciphering the Codex's enigmatic text and performing the rituals within, they could transcend the limitations of humanity and become something more. To them, it was not just a book but a gateway to unimaginable power and unimaginable possibilities. The cult's obsession with the Codex grew, as they saw it as their only path to ultimate enlightenment and dominance over the world. They were willing to go to any lengths, sacrificing everything in their pursuit of the knowledge and abilities promised within its pages.

Their journey had taken them beneath the surface of the cult's veneer, revealing the hidden depths of its enigmatic history. The cult's malevolent agenda was akin to an intricate tapestry, woven from the threads of the past and present. The truth lay concealed beneath the surface, awaiting discovery.

Under the surface, they had uncovered a world of secrets and deceit, a tapestry of beliefs and practices that defied reason. The cult's past was a multilayered narrative, a tale of darkness and forbidden knowledge that had stayed buried for far too long. As the investigators delved deeper into the cult's history, they found themselves entangled in a web of ancient rituals and arcane symbols. Each layer they unraveled only revealed more questions and mysteries waiting to be solved. It became clear that the cult's malevolent agenda was not simply a product of modern times but rather a continuation of a sinister legacy that stretched back centuries. The hidden depths of their enigmatic history held the key to understanding their true intentions and the power they wielded.

Their purpose was unequivocal: to face the cult, disclose the truth, and save Emily from the abyss. The way ahead remained clouded in uncertainty, but they were steadfast in their decision to go. The cult's secrets were akin to buried treasure, awaiting unearthing, and they were committed to following the trail beneath the surface to its chilling denouement.

Chapter 11: The Cult's Dark Secrets

The Cult of the Lost has long been an elusive and sinister presence, avoiding the grip of Detective James O'Connor and Detective Sarah Turner. As they pushed farther into the heart of this covert society, they were vividly aware that the moment had come to uncover its dark riddles and face the malevolence that had doggedly trailed their every step.

Their investigation voyage had directed them through a maze of intrigue, complicated relationships, and arcane information. Yet the crux of the cult's evil mission remained enshrouded in darkness. The cult's ancient knowledge resembled a tightly sealed vault, and they were adamant in their mission to get the elusive key that would open it. Determined to unravel the cult's secrets, they delved deeper into their research, consulting experts and poring over ancient texts. The more they discovered, the more they realized that the key to unlocking the cult's evil mission lay hidden within a web of cryptic symbols and coded messages. As they deciphered each clue, a sense of urgency grew within them, knowing that time was running out to prevent the malevolence from spreading further into society.

James and Sarah, immersed in their covert positions, had succeeded in establishing confidence inside the inner sanctuary of the cult. It was inside these hallowed meetings that they started to receive brief glimpses of the cult's ancient secrets, shrouded beneath a mask of ritualistic intensity.

The cult's rituals took on the aspect of a macabre theater, while members chanted incantations and choreographed strange procedures that hinted at distant regions and restricted knowledge. It was as if they had transcended into a region of the supernatural, where the barrier between truth and illusion blurred and the illusive tapestry of the cult's esoteric secrets started to take shape.

Their knowledge of the organization's ancient secrets improved as they uncovered a trail of disappearances inevitably tied to the group over decades. It was a legacy of split lives and destroyed families, an uncanny witness to the cult's malevolence. The cult's ancient mysteries cast a long and terrible shadow on the lives of its unlucky victims.

Father Malachai, the cult's mysterious head, stood as the protector of these esoteric mysteries, a steward of forbidden knowledge carried throughout centuries. His charm and authoritative air functioned as a cover, masking his actual nature—a skilled manipulator who kept his acolytes in a captivating grip. It was as if he had harnessed the arcane skills to serve the cult's mission.

Their adventure to expose the cult's unfathomable secrets led them to a subterranean library nestled inside the cult's stronghold, a convoluted storehouse of dusty tomes and timeworn manuscripts. It was a realm where history and the present mingled effortlessly and the boundaries between reality and the supernatural blurred. The cult's ancient secrets sat buried beneath, analogous to a reservoir of forbidden information awaiting discovery.

The portal to the cult's esoteric secrets was a tome known as the "Blackwood Codex," an old and prohibited text thought to store the cult's most jealously guarded information. This dreadful grimoire functioned as a portal to a world teeming with supernatural forces and arcane rites, a collection of the cult's credos and activities. It comprised the figurative Rosetta Stone that would uncover the convoluted intricacies of the cult's archaic secrets.

As they pored over the pages of the Blackwood Codex, James and Sarah were struck by the uncanny connections between the cult's esoteric secrets and the forbidden knowledge of old sagas and folklore. The codex reflected a modern-day interpretation of these age-old ideas, an evolutionary continuation of a heritage handed down through the annals of time.

The cult's ancient secrets were similar to an elaborate jigsaw puzzle—a complicated tale intertwined with perplexing rites and incantations that defied ordinary reasoning. It established a universe where the borders between the physical and the supernatural were blurred and where the cult's sway reached into the very fabric of reality.

Their purpose was unequivocal: to face the cult, disclose its archaic secrets, and rescue Emily from the abyss. The way ahead was perilous, but they realized that there could be no turning back. The cult's ancient secrets were similar to a cloak that had covered the truth for far too long, and they were devoted to carrying their purpose through to its terrible end. With each step they took, the air grew heavy with an otherworldly presence, as if the cult's influence was seeping into their very souls. The weight of their mission pressed upon them, fueling their determination to unravel the mysteries that lay ahead and free Emily from the clutches of darkness.

The cult's unfathomable mysteries resembled a maze of darkness—a frightening trek into the unknown. Nevertheless, James and Sarah were relentless in their mission to travel these hallways, to open the vault containing the cult's ancient secrets, and to face the malevolence that had caught them in this horrific domain of intrigue and deception.

Chapter 12: The Final Showdown

The time has come for Detective James O'Connor and Detective Sarah Turner to face the Cult of the Lost in a decisive showdown—a fight of intellect and resolve that would not only define the destiny of Emily but also lay bare the ancient mysteries that the cult had concealed for millennia. The scene was precisely prepared, and the stakes had never been greater.

Their quest had carried them deep into the center of the cult's cryptic domain, revealing the hidden verities that had escaped them for so long. The cult's evil objective was now disclosed, and the moment had come to directly face it, to unveil the maleficence that had entangled them in this realm of riddle and intrigue.

The final battle was analogous to a high-stakes game of chess, with each move methodically calculated and loaded with hazards. Father Malachai, the cult's mysterious leader, had shown himself a skilled manipulator, a puppeteer expertly tugging the threads of his disciples. Yet, James and Sarah were no longer players in his intrigues; they were adamant in their quest to challenge his domination, expose the cult's mysterious truths, and return Emily from the abyss.

As they entered the cult's inner circle, the ultimate confrontation developed into a sophisticated dance of deceit. They had to retain their cover and continue to earn the faith of the cult's believers while surreptitiously eroding its rule. The cult's rituals and congregations became the battlefield where truth struggled with deceit.

The ultimate confrontation was similar to an oncoming storm—a clash of conflicting forces that would determine the destiny of their lives.

The cult's mysterious secrets were the ultimate reward, and James and Sarah were clear in their intention to achieve them.

This climax also acted as a crucible of resolve, a furnace of challenges that would test their limitations. The cult's power and influence were tremendous, and its devotion to its sinister objective was steadfast. However, James and Sarah were spurred by an unrelenting resolve and an insatiable eagerness to rejoin Emily and battle the darkness that had constantly clouded their path.

The last battle was a collision of ideologies, a face-off exceeding the confines of reason. The cult's concern with parallel realms and arcane knowledge was at variance with the investigators' logical reality. This conflict was one between light and obscurity, truth-seeking versus the appeal of the mysterious.

The last showdown resembled a lighted fuse, and the tension in the environment was apparent. As they probed further into the cult's procedures, they revealed a world of ideas and rituals that appeared to defy the standards of rationality. The cult's rites were like scenes from a melancholy opera, a place where the borders between truth and illusion blurred and where the separation between the magical and the every day became vague.

This confrontation was also a meeting with history, a reckoning with the past that had molded the cult's mysterious mysteries. The Blackwood Codex, the ancient and outlawed text containing the secret to the cult's ideas and activities functioned as the bridge connecting the present to the past. It was a relic from a bygone period, a portal to the realm of forbidden knowledge buried through the years.

The last clash symbolized a test of heroism and faith in the quest for justice. The cult's enigmatic secrets were comparable to a web ensnaring them, yet they remained resolute to break free from its clutches.

This last meeting was analogous to a crossroads, where the pathways of destiny intersected. James and Sarah stood ready to tackle the impending challenges, negotiate the hazardous passages of the cult's domain, and combat the malevolence that had led them into this captivating story.

The ultimate battle was their moment of truth, a climactic chapter in an unyielding saga. The cult's mysterious secrets were similar to a buried gem waiting to be found, and they were firm in their devotion to carry their purpose through to its terrifying finish.

The ultimate encounter stood as a test of their mettle, a struggle that would define their destiny. The cult's control and authority were tremendous, but they stayed resolute in their desire to confront whatever obstacles lay ahead, to disclose the truth, and to reclaim Emily from the abyss. The moment for the last fight had come, and it was time for James and Sarah to challenge the Cult of the Lost, unveil its mysterious secrets, and bring this horrific saga to its finale. The stakes were at their height, the suspense was great, and the last battle would be a defining event, shaping the trajectory of their destiny.

Chapter 13: Redemption's Price

The long-anticipated last clash with the Cult of the Lost had come, and it was a fight that would take a toll. Detective James O'Connor and Detective Sarah Turner had crossed a treacherous path, revealing the cult's enigmatic secrets and facing its malevolence. However, the cost of redemption was about to be exposed, and it was considerably greater than they had thought.

As they penetrated the inner sanctuary of the cult, the tension in the air was tangible, like an oncoming storm set to release its turbulent wrath. The cult's rituals and congregations had morphed into a battleground—a stage where veiled truths contended with creative lies. It became a sophisticated dance of deceit, a high-stakes gamble where the prized reward was the cult's cryptic secrets.

Father Malachai, the cult's mysterious leader, appeared as a dangerous adversary—an accomplished manipulator who had carefully controlled the moves of his followers. His power operated as a cloak covering his actual character, and his magnetism was a weapon that had hooked the cult's followers. Yet, James and Sarah were no longer puppets in his vast game; they were steadfast in their mission to challenge his domination, uncover the cult's buried realities, and return Emily from the abyss.

This last encounter was a crucible, an assessment of their bravery and belief. The cult's power and control were tremendous, and their allegiance to its malicious mission was unshakable. Nonetheless, James and Sarah were spurred by an uncompromising resolve and an unquenchable yearning to rejoin Emily and face the darkness that had constantly overshadowed their path.

The battle was also a confrontation with history, a reunion with the past that had created the cult's enigmatic secrets. The Blackwood Codex, an ancient and outlawed text, contained the secret to the cult's beliefs and activities and acted as a conduit connecting the present to the past. It was a relic from a bygone period, a gateway to the realm of forbidden knowledge buried over the generations.

As they met the cult's inner circle, they couldn't help but be impressed by the similarities between the cult's guarded secrets and the forbidden knowledge of old stories and folklore. The codex arose as a modern interpretation of these age-old ideas, a continuation of a tradition handed down through the past.

The last clash was a test of their mettle, a struggle that would set the trajectory of their destiny. The cult's mysterious secrets had captured them like a web, but they remained firm in their quest to break free from its confines.

However, the cost of redemption was about to be exposed. As James and Sarah fought the battle against Father Malachai and the cult's inner circle, they realized that the malevolence of the cult stretched deeper than they had ever anticipated. The dark objective of the cult expanded beyond its rituals and meetings, delving into the heart of the city's underground.

The ultimate finale showed a clash with a criminal group known as the Black Serpents—an alliance that the cult had created to achieve its sinister purpose. The Black Serpents were like a sinuous entity hiding in the shadows, a criminal organization functioning with brutal efficiency. Their involvement with the cult has permitted them to pursue unlawful operations with impunity, from extortion to money laundering.

As the climactic battle developed, James and Sarah recognized that the cost of redemption was the revelation of the cult's suppressed secrets, a disclosure that may herald the demise of not just the cult but also the criminal syndicate that had joined forces with it. It was a risky wager, a high-stakes game where the repercussions remained shrouded.

The last battle was a match that came with a price. As they battled the cult and the Black Serpents, the cost of salvation was brought to light. They had to traverse a treacherous road to reveal the cult's cryptic secrets and bring its malevolence to the surface. However, in doing so, they would also deconstruct the criminal empire that had collaborated with the cult, a discovery with far-reaching ramifications.

The cost of atonement was a chance of danger, the overhanging prospect of revenge, and the murky route beyond the ultimate battle. Yet James and Sarah were adamant; they had gone too far to turn back. The cost of redemption was great, but they were steadfast in paying it to uncover the truth and recover Emily from the abyss.

The last clash was a furnace of bravery and conviction, a duel of intellect and drive. The cost of redemption was high, but they were firm in their desire to carry their mission through to its terrifying end. As they approached the cult and the Black Serpents at the zenith of their conflict, they were prepared to face whatever obstacles lay ahead, negotiate the hazardous passages of the cult's domain, and bring the riveting tale to its conclusion.

The price of redemption was a tremendous load to bear, but James and Sarah were eager to shoulder it. The last encounter was their moment of truth, a climactic chapter in a drama that had unfurled with unflinching resolve. The cost of redemption was steep, but the quest for truth was their ultimate aim, and they were steadfast in uncovering it, regardless of the price.

Chapter 14: Unearthing the Truth

The ultimate encounter had laid bare the intricate web of secrets and deceit that had enshrouded the Cult of the Lost. Detectives James O'Connor and Sarah Turner, unrelenting in their quest for truth and forgiveness, now faced the arduous challenge of digging into reality and disentangling the complex strands of the cult's terrible narrative.

As they looked more into the aftermath of the last encounter, it became obvious that the cost of redemption had been extravagant. The cult's malevolence had been revealed, its inner mechanics made naked, and its partnership with the Black Serpents had been sundered. Nonetheless, the aftermath resembled a storm—a swirl of confusion and uncertainty that threatened to consume them.

Unearthing the truth was a risky operation, analogous to a cautious excavation in a minefield of peril. The remains of the cult's influence nevertheless persisted, much like a toxic fog that hovered in the environment. James and Sarah had to proceed with care, negotiating the perilous environment as they strove to unearth the entire scope of the cult's dark secrets.

The Blackwood Codex, an old and illegal volume that contained the secret to the cult's beliefs and activities, stood as a beacon of outlawed knowledge. Its pages disclosed a universe of mystical energies and ancient ceremonies, an anthology of the cult's buried truths. Unearthing the truth requires rigorous inspection of the codex, a parsing of its obscure portions, and an investigation of the cult's hidden past.

The reality resembled a mosaic, a jigsaw puzzle of discoveries and secrets needing meticulous construction. James and Sarah methodically examined the cult's headquarters in search of buried papers, notebooks, and manuscripts that would provide insight into the cult's beginnings and its transformation. The truth reflected hidden riches awaiting excavation, and they were steadfast in their desire to discover them.

As they found the truth, they started to reveal the cult's links to a bigger network of esoteric groups, each with its evil objective. The cult had only been one component of a broader jigsaw, a cog inside a frightening worldwide machine. The reality resembled a spider's web, complicated and far-reaching, and they had to travel its strands to realize the entire depth of the cult's malevolence.

Unearthing the truth also led them to a trail of disappearances entangled with the cult for decades. The cult's dark objective had left behind a legacy of destroyed lives and divided families, with the echoes of their acts rippling through time. The reality was evocative of a haunting tune, a lament mirroring the cult's malevolence.

The truth also showed the breadth of Father Malachai's role in the cult's nefarious purpose. His function as a protector of forbidden information was important to their inquiry, and his charm and authority had been instrumental in enticing and maintaining cult members. The facts portrayed a master manipulator, someone who had adeptly twisted the strings of the cult's believers.

Unearthing the truth was not without its challenges. Former cult members, dissatisfied and horrified by the disclosures of its malevolence, had scattered like leaves in the wind. Many were unwilling to talk, weighed by fear of punishment or the embarrassment of their engagement in the cult's operations. The truth was a delicate relic, easily damaged, and they had to treat it with care.

As they proceeded to find the facts, they also revealed the cult's financial activities. The cult has been supported by an elaborate network of unlawful operations, including extortion, money laundering, and drug trafficking. The reality resembled a labyrinth of deceit, a domain of illicit activity that had fueled the cult's dark mission.

The truth was also the path to justice. James and Sarah engaged diligently with law enforcement organizations to guarantee that the cult's members suffered the ramifications of their conduct. The truth was similar to a sword, a weapon of justice that would cut through the darkness and take those guilty to account.

Unearthing the truth was a complicated and laborious quest, a painstaking examination of the cult's secret past. The truth paralleled buried riches awaiting exhumation, and James and Sarah were determined to carry their quest through to its terrifying end.

As the truth started to emerge, it functioned like a light piercing the darkness, illuminating the features of a world that had been shielded from view. Unearthing the truth was a monument to their unyielding tenacity and their devotion to justice and atonement. The truth had a cost; however, it was a price they were willing to endure to reconcile with Emily and face the darkness that had constantly darkened their path.

Unearthing the truth was their final act of atonement, the conclusion of their steadfast pursuit of justice. The truth resembled a light of clarity, illuminating the road that had brought them through the maze of lies and intrigue. As they proceeded to find the truth, they were steadfast in their quest to bring the cult to justice and to end this fascinating tale.

Chapter 15: The Lost Girl's Legacy

As the dust cleared from the disclosures and the realities that had been revealed, the legacy of the Lost Girl, Emily, cast a powerful shadow. Her adventure from innocence to the heart of evil had imprinted an unforgettable impact on all who had sought to save her. The legacy she left behind stood as a tribute to the irrepressible tenacity of the human spirit.

The legend of The Lost Girl braided its complex thread through the lives of Detectives James O'Connor and Sarah Turner. Their unflinching drive and tireless pursuit had uncovered the complex web of secrets and deceit constructed by the mysterious Cult of the Lost. Emily's legacy reverberated as a reflection of their unshakable devotion to justice and their effort to rescue her from the abyss.

The legacy of the Lost Girl was also a monument to redemptive power. Emily's journey had spanned regions of darkness and sorrow, but it also bore the mark of persistence and hope. Her power to survive the horrors of the cult's evil goal stood as a monument to the strength of the human spirit. Her legacy was analogous to a phoenix emerging from the ashes, representing rebirth and regeneration.

As the truth began to surface, it became obvious that Emily's legacy was not only personal but a communal one. The disclosures of the cult's actions sent reverberations across the community, motivating several former members to go forward and share their accounts. Emily's legacy became a rallying cry, inspiring others to face the darkness that had long tormented their lives.

The legacy of the Lost Girl also included a confrontation with the past. The malevolence of the cult had created a path of damaged lives and ruined families, and the legacy of their crimes could not be obliterated. Nonetheless, by bringing the cult to court and revealing its perplexing secrets, James and Sarah took a key step toward closure. Emily's legacy supplied a balm for the wounds of the past, functioning as a comforting salve for lasting anguish.

The legacy of the Lost Girl also highlighted the everlasting strength of love. Emily's abduction had troubled her father, James, and her sister, Sarah, for years. Their dogged effort to pull her back from the abyss and face the darkness that had overtaken her stood as a tribute to the fundamental links of family and the remarkable power of love. Emily's legacy shined as a light of hope, a heartbreaking reminder that love could transcend even the worst of situations.

The legend of the Lost Girl also acted as a cautionary tale. It remained a sharp warning of the hazards of deception and extremism. The cult's evil mission had trapped weak victims, luring them down a road of darkness. Emily's legacy operated as a warning, acting as a reminder that unrelenting vigilance was vital to defend against the enticing appeal of malicious powers.

The legacy of the Lost Girl was a monument to the endurance of the human spirit, a reflection of the eternal power of love, and a reminder of the requirement for unrelenting vigilance in the face of evil. It was a legacy that had affected the lives of many, inspiring them to face the darkness that persisted in their own lives.

As the tale of the Lost Girl's legacy came to a climax, James and Sarah were fully aware that their trip was far from its completion. The memory of the Lost Girl had become linked with their own, serving as a tribute to their unyielding devotion to justice and their persistent quest for truth. Emily's legacy shined like a flame, illuminating the darkest parts of their world, and they were committed to carrying it forward, ensuring her tale would not fade into oblivion.

The memory of the Lost Girl served as a reminder that the quest for justice was an endless adventure, one that took unyielding dedication and a constant commitment to exposing the truth. Emily's legacy served as a touchstone, signifying the eternal power of love and the tenacity of the human spirit. As they resumed their route, they carried the memory of the Lost Girl with them, a reminder that the pursuit of justice was a noble undertaking capable of lighting even the darkest of roads.

Milton Keynes UK
Ingram Content Group UK Ltd.
UKHW040706201123
432908UK00001B/149